Baby Cakes

New Year's Confetti Fun Cake

Author
Lisa Renee Hutchins

Illustrator
Rob Rice

Copyright 2024 Lisa Renee Hutchins

IBSN: 978-1-959446-20-0

Author

Lisa Renee Hutchins

Formatting By

Rob Rice

Illustrations and Cover Designs by

Rob Rice Illustrations

Editing by

Coronda Taliaferro, Luke Moyer, Jennifer Onishi, And Mike Arnone

All rights reserved. No part of this book may be reproduced or transmitted in any form or by any means, electronic or mechanical, including photocopying or recording, or by any information storage or retrieval system, without written permission from the publisher.

Published by

SRC Imagery LLC

This Baby Cakes book belongs to:

_____

I love the month of January! It means a new year and new beginnings for everyone.

Our family starts the new year off with writing a resolution, which is a goal you want to reach during that year.

My mom helps me write my resolution. We use colorful crayons and paper. Purple and pink are my favorite colors.

My brother Jordan can write his resolution all by himself.

His favorite colors are red and blue.

This year I will learn my ABC's!

Summer

My resolution is to learn my ABCs.

I will learn more about planes this year!

Jordan

Jordan's resolution is to learn about planes.

He will read a new book about planes every month.

It helps us remember our resolution goals.

Next, we clean up the table and get ready to make a New Year's Confetti Fun Cake!

The cool thing about this cake is the cake mix and frosting are filled with confetti sprinkles you can eat.

My job is to get out the mixing bowls.
Jordan's job is to get out the ingredients.

After the cake cools, our mom spreads frosting between the cake layers to make them stick together.

Finally, our mom covers the rest of the cake with frosting. It looks sprinkly delicious!

After our mom is done frosting the cake, she cuts us each a big piece of it and we all eat together.

The cake is so yummy!

New Year's Confetti Cake Checklist

Follow the baking directions on the back of the cake mix box and use the checklist below:

- 1 box of confetti cake mix
- Mixing and measuring utensils
- Mixing bowls
- 2 round cake pans
- 1 container of confetti frosting
- 1 container of pink frosting

Optional: Add 1 extra egg for additional moisture

Let's bake a cake!

Thank You

Dear Kiddos,

Hi, I am Lisa Renee Hutchins and I am excited to share my children's books with you! When I was a child, my mother always read my sister and I a story before bedtime, which is a tradition I continued when I had children. It brought us closer together and taught us new things.

Another tradition my family had was baking cakes for holidays, birthdays, and special occasions. It was fun and tasty!

I look forward to sharing with you my books about different children, their families' traditions, and cake recipes. Have fun reading and baking with someone you love!

Dear Parents and Caregivers,

Thank you for spending time reading and baking with your family! It is a great way to build lasting memories.

Author
Lisa Renee Hutchins

Connecting with Readers

My poetry and children's books, eBooks, and audiobooks can be found on Amazon, iTunes, and Audible.

Join me on social media!

Instagram: @thoughtsoflisarenee

Facebook, LinkedIn, and YouTube:
Author Lisa Renee Hutchins

Send me your thoughts at:
thoughtsoflisarenee@gmail.com

www.authorlisareneehutchins.com

About the Author

Lisa Renee Hutchins has been writing stories since she was a little girl. She loved the idea of taking people on a journey through a story.

She started publishing her poetry books in 2019 and has expanded her interest to writing children's books.

When she had children, there were not many books with characters that looked like her biracial children. That inspired her to write children's books that all kids could relate to and see themselves in. Exposing them to different types of families, cultures, races, traditions, and bringing them together through baking one of her favorite desserts… cake!

She hopes you enjoy learning about others and baking with someone you love!

About the Illustrator

Rob Rice has been an illustrator and animator since graduating from the Art Institute in Chicago, Illinois, in 2008. He loves to bring stories to life that build character and inspire readers to feel good about themselves and accomplish great feats.

In 2017, Rob had his greatest challenge yet. He lost his dominant right hand in an accident. He then taught himself how to draw and paint with his left hand and was able to continue to do what he loves.

Never give up on what you love!

Milton Keynes UK
Ingram Content Group UK Ltd.
UKHW051136021224
451508UK00022B/64